MAMA REX AND T
Run out of Tape

by Rachel Vail
illustrations by Steve Björkman

SCHOLASTIC INC.
New York Toronto London Auckland Sydney
Mexico City New Delhi Hong Kong

To Mom and Dad,
who taught me about giving.
—RV

For Gracie with love
—SB

ISBN 0-439-19920-4

Text copyright © 2001 by Rachel Vail.
Art copyright © 2001 by Steve Björkman.

12 11 10 9 8 7 6 5 4 3 2   1 2 3 4 5 6 7/0

Book design by Cristina Costantino

Printed in the U.S.A.
First Scholastic printing, January 2001

Contents

Chapter 1
THE HOLIDAY SPIRIT

Mama Rex and T walked into the brightness of a huge store. It seemed like the whole world was in there with them.

Mama Rex and T smiled at each other. They loved holiday time. In just a few hours, everyone they loved would be coming over to celebrate, so Mama Rex and T had to find a lot of perfect presents, fast.

Mama Rex asked, "What would you like, T?"

T had been hoping for that question. He led Mama Rex to Art Supplies, and pointed at the Deluxe Pack of Stickers.

T's best friend, Walter, had the Deluxe Pack of Stickers. Walter saved them for his most special art projects. He had given T a hologram sticker once, on T's birthday, but that was it.

T wanted his own Deluxe Pack, with sparkles and holograms all for himself.

"Please?" T chewed on his claw while Mama Rex read the back.

"We'll see," said Mama Rex, and placed the Deluxe Pack in the cart.

T was so excited he could hardly keep his tail from flomping.

"What do you want, Mama Rex?" he managed to ask.

"Bubble gum," Mama Rex answered.

"Really?" asked T.

"I haven't had any since the Cretaceous Period," said Mama Rex. "And I've really been wanting some."

"Interesting," said T.

They found the candy aisle. Mama Rex pulled down a box of bubble gum.

T looked at the back. "We'll see," said T, and placed the box of bubble gum into the cart.

Mama Rex and T went up and down aisles, carefully choosing presents for all their friends.

At first it was wonderful.

Soon it was not. There were too many colors, too much noise, and not enough air.

A girl grabbed a ball out of T's hand and ran away yelling, "MINE!"

The girl's father raced after her and on the way bonked Mama Rex's head with a tube of wrapping paper.

"This is a battle," whispered T.

"I need a large coffee," said Mama Rex. She turned the cart around and whispered, "Let's go."

T wilted against the cart while they waited in a long line. "How much longer?" asked T.

"Count," suggested Mama Rex.

T counted the things in the rack beside him. There were fourteen kinds of batteries. There were twenty kinds of candy. There was tape.

"Can we buy some tape?" asked T.

"No," said Mama Rex.

"To wrap the presents," explained T. "We'll need lots of tape."

"We have tape." Mama Rex checked her watch.

The cart behind them slammed into Mama Rex's back.

Nobody said "excuse me."

Mama Rex started breathing through her nose.

T wanted to explain why they needed more tape but he knew it was not a good idea to explain things while Mama Rex was breathing through her nose.

Mama Rex started unloading their things onto the counter.

"We might run out," T couldn't help whispering. "I think we might really need more tape."

Mama Rex slammed down the Deluxe Pack of Stickers. "Not. One. More. Thing," growled Mama Rex.

"But—" said T.

"Do NOT even say the WORD *tape!*" snarled Mama Rex.

"Ever again?" asked T.

Mama Rex closed her eyes.

T stopped looking at the tape. He helped unload the cart.

He waited with the bags on the sidewalk while Mama Rex hailed a cab.

T didn't say "tape" the whole way home. He talked about the snow instead.

T followed Mama Rex across their lobby and into the elevator. He pressed the button for their floor and leaned against the wall.

T dragged a bag down the hall and waited while Mama Rex unlocked their door.

He didn't mention tape at all.

Chapter 2
A Sticky Situation

Mama Rex and T had wrapped seventeen presents.

Thirty-one presents were waiting.

Mama Rex was using smaller and smaller bits of tape.

On the eighteenth present, the last piece of tape came off the roll.

"There must be more tape here somewhere," said Mama Rex.

Mama Rex opened every drawer in the kitchen.
She searched through T's art case.
She emptied her tool box.
No tape.
She cleared off the top shelf of the coat closet.
She dumped out her briefcase.
She rummaged around in the refrigerator.
She found half a bologna sandwich but no tape.

"Wait a sec!" yelled Mama Rex. She ran to her bedroom.

T followed Mama Rex.

Mama Rex was throwing pocketbooks out of her closet onto the floor.

All T could see was the tail of Mama Rex, and flying pocketbooks.

"Aha!" yelled Mama Rex. She backed out of the closet.

In one of her hands was a yellow pocketbook.

In the other hand was a half-used, linty roll of tape.

"Hooray!" yelled T.

T followed Mama Rex back to the living room.
They taped and folded and cut.
They turned on festive music and sang along in loud voices.

Until they ran out of tape again.

"We'll find more," said Mama Rex. "I know there must be more."

Mama Rex unmade her bed.
She emptied the dishwasher.
She plunged the toilet.
No tape.

She emptied the saltshaker.

She dug through the garbage.

She flung everything out of T's underwear drawer.

She found two uncapped markers, forty-seven cents, six fossils, and a flamingo.

But no tape.

No tape anywhere.

Mama Rex made some hot chocolate.

T floated mini-marshmallows in it.

Mama Rex and T sipped from steaming mugs, looking out the window. The snow was coming down even harder than before. The sky was darkening into evening.

"What are we going to do?" asked T.

Their apartment didn't look ready for the party anymore.

After a few minutes, Mama Rex started to smile. "I have an idea," she said.

Chapter 3
GIFTS

Mama Rex held up the box of bubble gum.

"That's your present," said T. "You're not supposed to see it yet."

"Bubble gum is sticky," said Mama Rex.

"So?" T asked.

"So we need something sticky," explained Mama Rex. "Right?"

"Ew, disgusting," said T.

Mama Rex smiled. "Yeah, but what else can we do?"

T took the box of bubble gum from Mama Rex
and hid it behind his back. "Forget," he said.

"Forget what?" asked Mama Rex.

"Good," said T, and slowly spread his arms. In
one hand, he held the box of bubble gum.

He lifted the box toward Mama Rex.

Mama Rex opened her mouth wide. "For me?" she asked.

T nodded.

Mama Rex jumped up and down, hugging the box.

"You like it?" T asked.

"Just what I wanted," said Mama Rex.

Mama Rex tore open the box. She pulled out two pieces of gum and handed one to T.

"Thanks," said T. He unwrapped his piece and popped it in his mouth.

Mama Rex and T chewed their gum. They blew a few bubbles.

"Now let's see if this works," said Mama Rex.

Mrs. Himmelfarb's present lay half-wrapped on the table.

Mama Rex took the wad of gum out of her mouth.

Thwak! Mama Rex stuck the gum to the wrapping paper and folded the edges up.

"It works!" yelled T.

Mama Rex and T each chewed nineteen pieces
of gum. Luckily, they had very powerful jaws.
T shook the bubble gum box. No gum fell out.
They had chewed up Mama Rex's whole present,
and there were still seven boxes to wrap.

Mama Rex flopped onto her chair, with her tongue hanging out. "Well," she said. "Some guests will have to get unwrapped presents."

T sank down in his chair to think. After a minute, T said, "I have an idea."

T went to the pile of presents and pulled out the Deluxe Pack of Stickers.

"No, T," said Mama Rex. "You don't have to."

"It's OK," said T.

"You're the one who said we need tape," said Mama Rex. "I should have listened to you."

"Yeah," said T. He held the Deluxe Pack of Stickers out to Mama Rex.

"But you'll use them up," said Mama Rex.

"I'll be using them with you," said T. "That's what I wanted them for anyway."

Mama Rex hid the stickers behind her back, then slowly spread her arms. She handed the stickers to T.

"Just what I wanted," whispered T.

T hugged his gift, then tore it open and spread the sheets of stickers on the table.

"Help yourself," T told Mama Rex.

Mama Rex hugged T. "You are so special," she said.

Mama Rex and T wrapped the rest of the presents.

They got ready for their party.

Some of the guests were very surprised when they opened their gifts. But they were all happy with what they got.

Especially Mama Rex and T.